Daisy's day at the Seaside

Christine & Olive

Daisy's day at the Seaside

MYRIAD BOOKS LIMITED

MYRIAD BOOKS LIMITED
35 Bishopsthorpe Road, London SE26 4PA

First published in 1995 by
MIJADE PUBLICATIONS
16-18, rue de l'Ouvrage
5000 Namur-Belgium

Translation: Lisa Pritchard

ISBN 1 84746 040 2

Printed in China

All summer, Daisy the cow has been deep in thought. She really wants to see the sea. After all, Danny the dog has been to the seaside with his owner.

But whoever heard of a farmer taking his cow to the seaside?

Daisy is so sad. "It's too far to walk!"

Danny starts to cry too. And so does Cloud.

"Oh Cloud, you are so lucky! You can just float wherever you want."

"It's true," says Cloud, "I've seen the sea, and the mountains, lakes and forests."

"Wow," says Daisy. "That's amazing."

"I've got a good idea," says Cloud.
"I'm going to take you on a trip
you'll never forget. Jump on and hold
on tight!"

Daisy and Danny take a good look
around. What a long way down!

And look over there – what's that
blue line?

"It's the sea! I can see the sea!"

Daisy rolls in the sand and jumps in
the waves. Meanwhile, Cloud is up
to something…

"Hop on!" Cloud says.

"Faster, faster!" shouts Daisy.

Cloud speeds up, swerving this way
and that way. Daisy and Danny love
it. They are all having a great time.

"Come and play ball," Danny calls. But Daisy's fast asleep. Cows like to have a nap in the middle of the day.

Later on Daisy goes swimming.
It's such fun being a mermaid! And
down here nobody can splash you…

All that fun has made everyone hungry. There's just time to have an ice-cream. Then it's time to go home.

Cloud floats along quietly. Daisy and Danny are fast asleep.

Back in their field, Cloud gently wakes them up. They say goodbye and he floats off.

"What an amazing day!" says Daisy.